Tom's Tree

Gillian Shields

illustrated by
Gemma Raynor

GULLANE
CHILDREN'S BOOKS

Tom planted a seed.
'That won't grow,' laughed
his big brother Ned.

'I think it will,' said Tom. 'It will . . .

. . . grow into a tree with
strong green branches and
golden leaves and
red fruit and
peacocks singing.'

'Peacocks don't sing,' said Ned.

The next day, Tom looked where he had
planted the seed. There was no tree growing.
'Let's play football,' said Ned.

But Tom was thinking about his tree.
'When my tree grows,' he said, 'we can . . .

. . . build a tree house
like a pirate ship and
fly over the moon.'

'Trees can't fly,' said Ned.

Every day, Tom looked to
see if his tree was growing.
But the ground was
bare and empty.

'I told you so,' said Ned.
Tom was sad.
'My tree would have been . . .

. . . as tall as a giant,
as wide as a rainbow and as strong as a dragon.'

'Dragons don't exist,' said Ned.

So Tom stopped hoping.

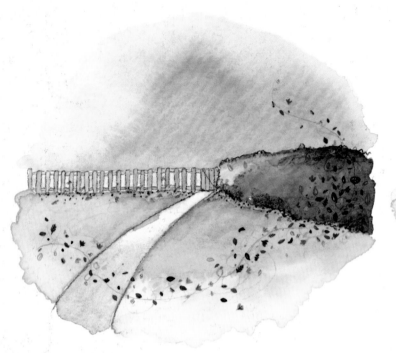

Then the winds came . . .

and the rain came . . .

and the snow and the frost,

until one day, the sun shone again . . .

. . . and the spring had come back.
'Look, Tom, look!' said Ned.
'It's your tree.'

Tom smiled at Ned. Ned smiled at Tom.

'Pirates!'
'Dragons!'
'Rainbows!'
'Giants!'

'But,' said Tom, looking at his tree again, 'it's very small.'
'Don't worry, it will soon grow,' said Ned.

So Tom looked after
the tiny tree and watered it.

He built a little fence around it,
so it wouldn't get damaged.

He watched and waited as a new shoot grew, and fresh green buds opened.

At night, Tom looked out of his
window into the darkness of the garden.
Sometimes, he thought he could hear the
mast of a tall ship creaking in the wind,
and the faint, soft sound of peacocks
singing under the starlight.

But every morning Tom's tree seemed as small as ever.
'I wish you'd hurry up,' said Tom to the tree.

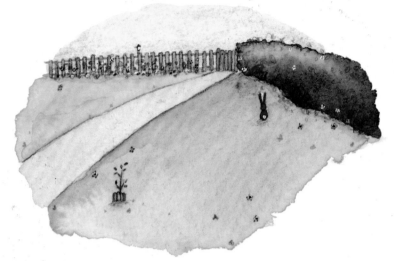

Spring followed spring.

Summer followed summer.

At last, the tree grew, but Tom grew faster.

The day came when Tom was all grown up. He didn't think about pirates and dragons any more. He went away to have grown-up adventures instead. The young slim tree sighed in the breeze.

One day, a man walked through the garden gate, down
the path and stood in front of the tree. It was Tom.
He was carrying his son on his shoulders.
'Look, Edward,' said Tom. 'This is my tree.'
The tree was tall and wide, with strong green branches.

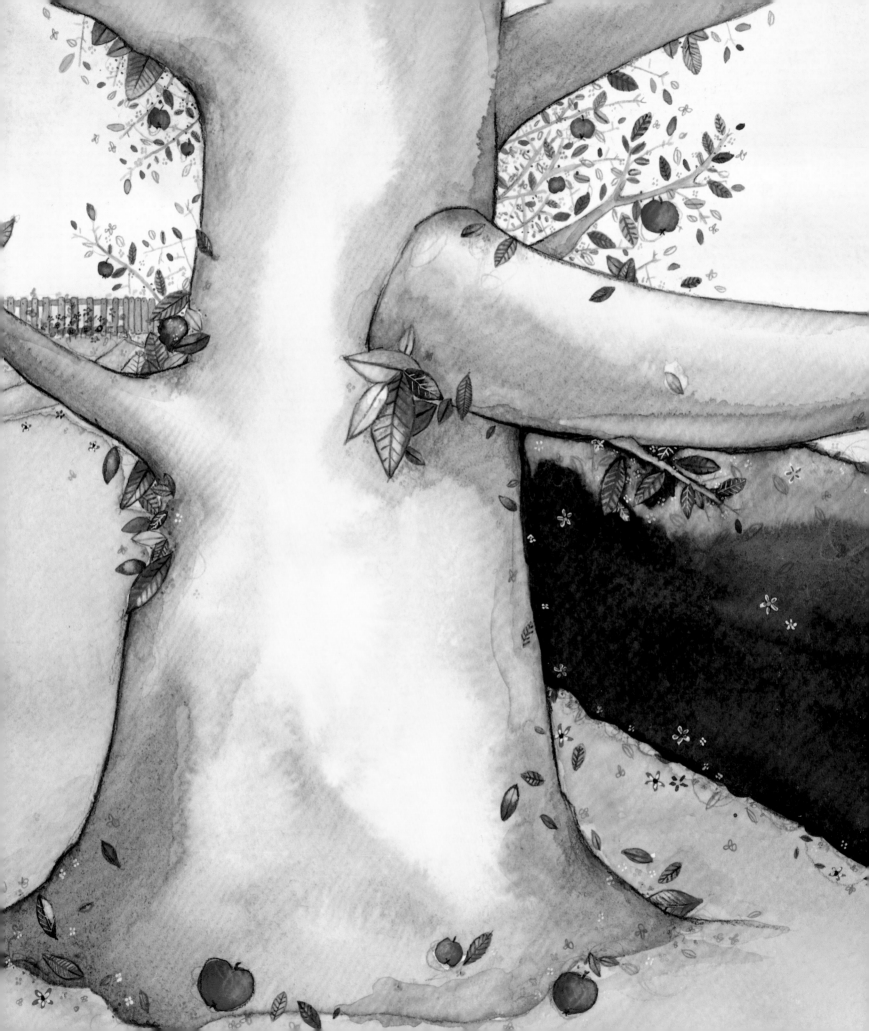

Edward looked up.
He laughed and clapped his hands. He could see the
tall mast of a ship, and
juicy red fruit, and
little golden dragons hiding in the leaves.
And high up in the branches he could see
glittering green peacocks.

He could see
Tom's tree.
And the tree laughed in the rustling wind.

Other
Gullane Children's Books
for you to enjoy…

Holly's Red Boots
Francesca Chessa

Ferdie and the Falling Leaves
by Julia Rawlinson
illustrated by Tiphanie Beeke

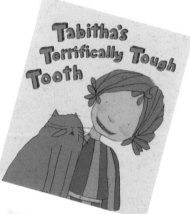

The Secret To Teddy's Happiness
by David Conway
illustrated by Dubravka Kolanovic

Tabitha's Terrifically Tough Tooth
Charlotte Middleton

Lucy and the Bully
Claire Alexander

Small Florence
Claire Alexander